Copyright © 2019 Clavis Publishing Inc., New York

Originally published as *Mijn mama en ik* in Belgium and Holland by Clavis Uitgeverij,
Hasselt—Amsterdam, 2018
English translation from the Dutch by Clavis Publishing Inc., New York

Visit us on the Web at www.clavis-publishing.com.

My Mommy and Me written and illustrated by Liesbet Slegers

ISBN 978-1-60537-452-9

This book was printed in January 2019 at Wai Man Book Binding (China) Ltd. Flat A, 9/F., Phase 1,
Kwun Tong Industrial Centre, 472-484 Kwun Tong Road, Kwun Tong, Kowloon, H.K.

First Edition
10 9 8 7 6 5 4 3 2 1

Liesbet Slegers

My Mommy
and Me

Clavis

NEW YORK

This is my mommy.

Mommy and I love playing together.

Hide-and-seek is fun!

What do we do when she finds me?

My mommy and I

This is my mommy.

We work in the backyard together.

She mows the lawn.

And I water the plants.

My mommy and I ...

This is my mommy.

We shop for school clothes together.

We go to the shoe store.

My mommy and I

... both love
new shoes.

This is my mommy.

We go to the beach together.

She carries our things.

I run ahead.

My mommy and I ...

This is my mommy.

Mommy and I look in the mirror.

It's almost time for bed.

What do we do first?

My mommy and I ...

... both love to take a bath.

This is my mommy. Mommy loves
to cuddle. She reads me a story.
And then it's time for bed.

My mommy and I ...

... love each other very much.